MARY

CATCHING UP

RICHARD LEE

Dedicated to a world in need of
love and imagination.

"You are never too old to become younger!"
- Mae West

CONTENTS

FOREWORD

The EROS CRESCENT novels take you on a journey like no other - to places you couldn't imagine - a female friendly sex club or a privately owned members-only dogging venue; the toy-boy life of a writer working on the Amalfi coast and much much more. *MARY* and the other novellas - *JESSICA, MARIA, HELEN, JANICE* and *THE CLUB* - are extracts taken from *The Fifi Code, Eros Crescent* and *Mount Eros*.

PREFACE

Mary sat looking gorgeous as only she could, her weight pushing out her stockings, her dress and blouse in Rubenesque splendour, and everything designed to precariously balance on her strappy high heels.

– from The Fifi Code

1

MARY

IT WAS Alice's birthday party night at No 17 Eros Crescent.

Alice's, stepmother Helen was just leaving a conversation with two couples; neighbours who lived either side of them.

"Ah! Here we are, the party girl herself. Alice, these are our neighbours Hilda and Charlie, who live at number nineteen, and Harold and Mary who live at number fifteen."

"Hello, Hilda and Charlie and hello, Harold and Mary. So glad you could come."

Harold seemed to be already a bit tipsy and Hilda tottered a little as she turned towards me and grinned rather grotesquely. They wished me a happy birthday.

Helen and Freya stopped making love only because Helen suddenly remembered that she was supposed to be the hostess to the party guests.

When the two women went inside the house, they discovered that there were only two couples still there and Helen was shocked at what was happening.

The husband of one couple had passed out, as had the woman from the other couple.

What was a surprise was that the two who had not got drunk to the point of oblivion had discovered each other and moved into the study, where they lay on the floor.

The buttocks of a very large woman were heaving and her fat legs were flaying about as in a soft voice she whispered, "Give it to me, give it to me Charlie, more, yes, that's it, more, fuck me you gorgeous bastard," followed by another quiet voice saying, "Oh Mary. I love you Mary. Here, have some more, Mary".

Helen looked shocked.

"Well, I would never have expected that sort of behaviour in our house. If that is not being neighbourly, I don't know what is."

Freya giggled.

"There must be something in the air, Helen?"

They both laughed and kissed.

A Thai meal was the right thing, and the Saturday evening meal together at Helen and Freddy's house at Eros Crescent was wonderful, and made even better with the good conversation and humorous banter.

Frederico was in good form, avoiding some of his pet topics, usually the sort that men like to use to show off their knowledge to one another. Subjects like the origins of Guinness stout, or ways of keeping planes in the air.

Helen had more exciting things to talk about. She had gossip.

"Come on, Helen. What has got you so fired up? Tell us please. We're bursting to know."

"Well, Alice, and you, Freya, the matter is a little sensitive to say the least, so what I say must not leave these four walls."

"Oh come on step-mum, you are driving us insane. Just say it."

"Freya, you will remember the night of Alice's birthday when we came into the house on our way to visit her and Freddy and our attention was caught by something that was happening in the study. We had already noticed that a man and woman had passed out drunk in the lounge.

"As we were passing the slightly open door of the study, we noticed a very large pair of women's knickers hanging on the door knob and we heard voices."

"Don't tell me you didn't look to see who it was, Helen?" Alice chipped in.

"Be quiet darling, we are not all perverts and voyeurs."

"Well, Freya and I did just have a peep to make sure that everything was all right, no one being murdered or anything.

"Anyway, everything seemed fine. We didn't stay long, did we Freya? Just long enough to see that Charlie from number nineteen was fully immersed in a private part of the very large Mary from number fifteen.

"As I said before, we didn't stay long, being in a hurry as we were to join you two in the bedroom. But it did seem that they were very pleased to be doing what they were doing, and Mary indicated that she would like to be doing this for ever and ever.

"We were not sure what his reply was, but we suspected his gurgling was in the affirmative."

Everyone screamed with laughter and Freya said how, with great difficulty, she had dragged Helen from the room. Helen pulled a face at her and she and Frederico laughed heartily.

"So! Has this story got a happy ending darling? Have they run off to the Caribbean together or something? Will we be getting new neighbours?"

There followed a general buzz of speculation. I thought that their respective partners should be involved, so that then all would be blameless.

Frederico suggested that partner swapping could become the new norm on the street and began naming neighbours whom he thought he could manage to get off with, to which Helen added her comments: "No, she's a bit of a bitch", or "No, she'd kill you" or, "Yes, Mr So-and-so in number so-and-so is rather interesting."

When they settled down, Freya asked a question.

"So Helen, can we help the lady with the giant knockers, I mean knickers, get more of dear Charlie?"

"A good question, darling. Yes, we can and I have. That is my news. You all need to know so that no one interrupts our lovers. I've given them both a key to the potting shed. As well, I've taken a spare mattress to the shed and some pillows.

Everyone clapped and raised their glasses and cheered, and called out "Well done, Helen."

"But what did they say? Did you seek them out separately? Were they shocked that you knew?"

"Well, I didn't see Charlie. I had seen Harold leaving with a car-load of mates to play golf, so I went in and saw Mary.

"And yes, she was shocked, but not as much as I thought she might be. She had a little cry and professed her undying love for Charlie.

"She was over the moon when I presented her with the keys. Now all she needs to do is simply text him, then nip through the side gate or over the fence and meet him there and give him a key. Bingo, big knickers can hang alongside the onions and the dahlia tubers. What better way to plant the life force?"

"And a happy ending all round, I presume. And we, darling, get our very own garden gnomes with extras."

"Yes, Frederico, and you only get peeping and perving rights, if we do it together."

Lots of hilarity followed and every aspect was discussed, even to concern about their respective spouses finding out.

"I must say that the other two are not especially likeable. He can be particularly rude and she is a snob par excellence. I doubt either has a loving bone in their body," said Helen.

"Now, darling, we mustn't judge them too harshly. Perhaps they just need to get out more."

"Perhaps they could get off together and you could give them keys to your studio?

"Then I could go down with trays of sandwiches and cupcakes and make a few bob. I could offer a shopping service so that they didn't have to stop. And of course, you will have a supply of nudes to paint."

Frederico was loving the story of the neighbours' follies, and milking it for all he could.

"Stop it, Frederico. We've done the neighbours now."

———

It was only a few weeks after Helen had played Good Samaritan and handed keys to the potting shed to Mary so that she and Charlie could meet to make love in secret, that Helen, passing the potting shed on her way to her studio, heard a muffled sound coming from within. It didn't sound like a couple making love; rather more like someone sobbing.

Helen stopped and wondered if she should investigate. If there was something going on between lovers, that was their affair, and she should not interfere. But she could hear only one person, and decided to knock and enter.

"Mary? Are you all right, darling?"

She heard Mary blow her nose and then, a few moments later, call out for her to come in.

Mary sat looking gorgeous as only she could, her weight pushing out her stockings, her dress and blouse in Rubenesque splendour, and everything designed to precariously balance on her strappy high heels.

"Darling Mary? What is wrong? Tell me?"

Mary said nothing, but simply passed her phone to Helen. Helen read the message:

So sorry my darling, Hilda has found out and is fearful of a scandal. We are already on a plane heading for an extended holiday on a cruise ship in Europe. She has arranged for number nineteen to be sold immediately we get back. Will be in touch. Much love, Charlie.

"Oh, Mary, you poor darling."

I sat on the bed beside her and wrapped my arms around the large lady. I could feel her shaking with emotion.

We must have sat like that for a good half hour, until Mary could cry no more.

Suddenly she gave a short little laugh.

"Well, Charlie gets a holiday in Europe out of it."

I giggled in response.

"But Mary, that is not what Charlie really wants. He wants to be here in your arms."

That opened the floodgates again.

When Mary had once again become silent, we just sat. Then I adjusted us both to be more comfortable and we lounged back against the pillows stacked against the wall behind us.

"I will especially miss the kissing," Mary squeaked.

After a few minutes of silence, I spoke.

"I think we could possible fix that. Well, sort of."

"What do you mean, Helen?"

I had one arm around her neck and my other arm and hand rested on her large thigh. Then I gently turned the hand over and began to rub her thigh through her skirt.

I drew Mary's head towards mine, and, lifting my hand from her thigh, I turned her face towards me. Mary's still wet eyes focused on my face and I smiled lovingly at her. Then I put my lips on hers, knowing that this could be a terrible mistake.

I left my lips on hers. She didn't immediately respond, but at least she hadn't pulled away.

I was ready to retreat and remove my lips, when suddenly Mary pushed back at me with her mouth, gently. I waited a moment, wanting to give her some space. Then she pushed at me harder.

I put my hand behind her head and pulled it slowly towards me while increasing the pressure on her lips. Then I took a risk and pushed my tongue into her mouth, just a tiny distance, and moved it slowly, side to side.

All of her body shook and as it subsided, I realised that Mary was experiencing a huge emotional release. But there must still have been some tension remaining. I could feel her looking for something, something more, looking for what I might do next.

I decided to take another risk.

I unbuttoned my blouse. I was without a bra and I felt the cool air on my breasts. I picked up Mary's right hand and slowly placed it inside my blouse and waited.

I felt Mary shaking and gasping as she hurriedly moved her hand around, feeling my skin and discovering a nipple. And while she was doing that, she picked up my spare hand and placed it against the exposed skin of her large bosom, and I gratefully slid my hand down inside her top. I too found a nipple and I too, gasped and sighed.

Then Mary began to moan and moved her mouth around on mine, and we both tongued each other.

"I want to help you get through this, Mary my darling. Please let me make love to you?"

I only had to wait a second or two before she answered.

"Oh yes, Helen, please, please make love to me. This all feels so wonderful, so right. Do whatever you want to me, Helen. Anything!"

I held her tight. Then I asked her to follow me to my studio just a few metres away, where we would be much more comfortable.

We stood up and moved to the studio.

We lay down on the big bed and made ourselves comfortable. Mary was desperate to keep kissing me and pawed at me to get to my lips. And when I let her, and our mouths were again fastened together, and we had each resumed our nipple play, I slowly moved my hand down to her crotch and lightly fingered her through her skirt.

"Oh Helen, this is heavenly," Mary whispered.

She reached down and drew up her skirt, then she took my hand and pushed it down into her knickers, placing it atop her huge pouting hairy pussy. We both gave an excited cry.

"Oh yes, Mary! That feels so good. Thank you, my darling."

"Helen, it belongs to you now. Your fingers feel wonderful. Do anything, darling. Whatever you want, and I will love and cherish you for it always."

I lifted my head and gazed down on Mary's enormous stockinged thighs and legs. Her suspenders rolled down and over her fleshy upper thigh, on their way to her stocking tops.

I knew what I wanted next. It was something that my true love, Alice and I shared a lust for: seeing a woman's stockinged legs and shoes waving in the air.

Holding Mary's legs up in the air and looking at them, while I shafted her with the big strap-on, hidden beneath the bed, would be so wonderful and sexy. And I believed Mary would enjoy it too.

As we kissed and I slowly rotated my hand on Mary's pussy, I reached down and brought out the strap-on from beneath the bed. I did not want to frighten her with it, so I knew she had to see it first.

"Mary darling, I've got a special thing that Frederico and I play with sometimes if he's feeling a little flat and I need his attention. Would you like to see it?"

Mary looked at me quizzically.

"What is it, Helen? Can you show me?"

I put the dildo slowly up to my mouth, watching her as I did so. Her eyes were suddenly wide open.

"Oh Helen, it's a giant cock."

I put out my tongue and started licking it, then I put the end into my mouth and as I did so, I lowered myself towards her mouth. I took it from my mouth and placed it next to hers.

"Lick if for me, darling."

Still looking amazed, Mary did not hesitate, quickly pushing out her tongue to touch it. I slowly rotated it and then gently pushed it between her lips. Almost in a trance, Mary opened her mouth and moved it forward, over the end of the dildo. I rocked it slowly backwards and forwards in her mouth, then I put her hand on it and asked her to hold it for me for a moment while I removed her knickers. Mary lifted herself so that I could more easily slide them off.

Then I took the dildo back and she watched, fascinated, as I buckled up the band around my waist.

"Helen? Will this feel like a real cock?"

I squeezed some lubricant into her vagina hidden amidst a jungle of curly hair. Then I placed the dildo against her and moved it slowly in, watching as I did so the magic of her vagina opening up to receive me. It was a beautiful sight.

"Is that okay, Mary? It's not uncomfortable in any way? Say if it is and I will stop immediately."

Mary's eyes were closed and her mouth was wide open. I heard a moaning sound, then suddenly Mary thrust herself up towards me and screamed "Yes, yes, oh Helen, yes!"

Mary had a new special friend, and I had a new lady-love.

I gave Mary a slow but serious shagging with the dildo and we both loved it. I would sometimes stop, but then the lower part of her body would thrust upwards and she would call out "More please Helen, more!"

Now I was ready. I wrapped a hand around each of her ankles, just above her bright blue high heels and lifted up her legs, speaking as I did so.

"Mary?"

"Yes, Helen?"

"Just so that you know. Having your beautiful stockinged legs and your shoes waving in the air in front of me fulfils a fantasy for me that cannot be beaten. If you ever feel that I'm not showing you enough attention, Mary, just say, 'I want my legs in the air please' and I will be your sex slave in seconds."

Mary giggled.

"Oh Helen. Everything about you is so beautiful. You shouldn't have told me that. I'll be texting you every day with that message. I will exhaust you."

We both laughed, then Mary went into a serious panting and groaning mode as I set about finishing off her first strap-on shagging, and with an orgasm that made her cry with happiness.

When we had finished and it was time for Mary to return home, she threw her arms about me and declared her love for me. Then as she was about to leave, she asked:

"Where can I get one of those, Helen? Just in case something was ever to happen to you."

We laughed and I promised to take her on a special shopping spree soon.

"There is another world out there Mary, and it is waiting for you."

The day after Mary and I had made love, I received a call from her telling me that Harold had been taken to hospital from the golf club after suffering a severe heart attack. He had died later that night.

Mary didn't sound particularly distraught. I was ready to rush over, then I figured that a lot had happened to her in a very short time, and she needed a quiet spell to digest it all.

"Mary? You must call me or just come over if you need to. Promise you will call?"

"Yes, Helen. Thank you. Love you."

I went and found Freddy and told him the news.

"I always knew that golf was bad for you," he quipped.

"She knows we're here for her, doesn't she darling?"

"Yes, sweetheart. She has promised to phone or come over if she needs us or wants company."

I hugged Frederico. I wonder if he knows how much I love him, I thought.

One afternoon, a couple of days after Mary called to tell me about Harold, she rang and asked if she could visit. I suggested she come for dinner and she said she had a niece visiting from the country and could she bring her along. I told her that would be fine.

Freddy answered the doorbell and I heard him offering Mary his commiserations. Then he ushered Mary and her niece into the dining room, where I was just finishing laying the table.

"Darling, Mary is here with her niece, Sophie. Sophie, this is Helen."

"Pleased to meet you, Helen. Auntie has talked about you a lot," said the young woman, staring intently at me with her very bright eyes.

I almost blushed. What had Mary said? I wondered. Sophie looked like what you might expect a young country girl to look like. Quite tall, fresh-faced and with a slightly naive or innocent expression permanently displayed. She was dressed modestly, with dark trousers and jacket and a simple button-up blouse, and she wore a pair of very sensible shoes.

"Lovely to meet you, Sophie. A sad time no doubt, but I'm sure Mary welcomes an opportunity to see you. You are from way up north, I believe. I hope you will be here for a while, so we get a chance to get to know you."

"Well, Auntie and I are still talking things through. She feels it could be time for me to leave the farm and spend time in the big city, and she's offered me accommodation if I choose to move down here."

"But do you think it's time to leave home Sophie? Don't let Mary talk you into it if it isn't what you want."

"Well, moving out is what I want, so Auntie doesn't really have to do much to persuade me. Being able to live at her house will make everything much easier."

I excused myself to go to the kitchen and check dinner and left Frederico to play host. When I returned, Freddy and Sophie were looking through the DVD's, hoping to find something that Mary would like to relax her after a gruelling week dealing with undertakers and funeral preparations.

I went over to Mary.

"Hello, darling. So good to see you."

"Thank you Helen. I've missed you."

"Sophie seems lovely. How old is she?"

"She turned twenty-two in July just gone. I think her moving to my place would be wonderful, don't you? She doesn't have a boyfriend where she lives, and there are very few young people left on the surrounding farms. I was surprised she was so happy to talk to you. She is usually very shy and rarely talks to people. Maybe having you and Frederico next door will be good for her. You do have a talent for relaxing people, I've noticed."

We both laughed at the innuendo in Mary's statement.

"Dearest Mary, are you OK? It must have been a shock."

"Better than I would have expected, darling. It is strange, and I can only say this to you, but the loss of Harold has been liberating. Already I'm feeling relaxed, knowing that I can do anything I want to, and when I want, and not be answerable to anyone."

I leant forward and kissed her lightly on the lips.

"Well, Mary, it is so good that you see it that way. I wonder what your new liberated life will bring and where it will take you? And of course, they say that good things come in threes. Hmm! Look out, girl! Don't go leaving me for a new hot love just yet. I'm not ready for that."

We both laughed, and I headed off to the kitchen.

"Frederico, will you be able to help me serve dinner, please?"

"Yes, darling, I'll be there in seconds."

On the following Monday, Mary phoned and said things were a bit hectic and she wouldn't be able to meet me the next day as planned.

Then she added that, because she wouldn't be able to make it and she didn't want me to be lonely, she was sending me a present and when I enquired what it was she told me that Sophie said she would happily stand in for her and that she had given her the new key, the one I had just given her for the studio.

I was taken aback a bit, and expressed my surprise and asked Mary what Sophie knew. She said she had told Sophie enough to get her excited. 'The rest is up to you, darling. I honestly want you both to have fun. She needs it, and you, darling Helen, in appreciation of your loving gift of liberation, deserve it."

I laughed and thanked her, reminding her that it was looking even more urgent that we go shopping, and for her to get that special thing, and to keep Friday free to do it if she could.

She laughed and said she would.

I was a little on edge as I walked to my studio. I really hadn't had time to get to know Sophie. I knew she was a very capable farm girl with no boyfriend, and that there were very few young people her age in the region. I also knew that she had a certain look which I liked, and that underneath her trouser pants I suspected she had a nice pair of legs.

I tapped on the studio door to let her know I was there, and went in.

Sophie stood tall on a pair of high heels that she had gone shopping for with Mary the day before. Her stockings were a delightful smoky grey and she wore a shortish but conservative pleated skirt and a blouse buttoned to a frilly lace collar. Her face still wore that naive expression that I noticed when first we met, but there was something else going on suggesting a not-so-innocent state of mind.

"Hello Sophie, and welcome."

Before I could say another word, Sophie crossed the room and threw her arms around me and fastened her mouth on mine. I slipped my arms around her and pushed back on her lips; then her mouth opened and she put out her tongue and explored my now open mouth. We stood like that for a few minutes, then I slid my hand down her back and lightly felt her backside.

We eventually separated our mouths and Sophie smiled.

"Auntie said it would be best if I kissed you straight away, then I wouldn't be so nervous."

I laughed and turned her towards the bed, and we sat down.

"Dearest Mary! Did her advice work, Sophie? You're no longer nervous, I hope?"

"Yes, Helen, I feel relaxed with you now. Do you like my shoes?"

"Good! Yes, I love your shoes. I do have a bit of a shoe and foot fetish. Now Sophie, can I please do something, so that I won't feel nervous?"

Sophie looked at me with eyes shining.

"Anything!" she whispered.

I slowly unbuttoned my blouse right the way down and pulled it open, then I took Sophie's hand and drew it over my bosom and rubbed her fingers lightly on my bare breast.

"Please find a nipple, Sophie, and lick it."

Her face was a picture of surprise, delight and then lust. She put up her other hand and moved her face to my breasts, and within moments was nipping and tugging me with both hands and her teeth.

"Oh, you darling girl. You've made me feel less nervous already," I whispered soothingly.

Sophie moved back and stared into my eyes.

"That's good, Helen. Can I keep playing with you breasts, or would you like me to do something else?"

"In a little while Sophie, you know that I will want to shag you. I'm about to take off your skirt, beautiful girl. I can't wait any longer."

Sophie whimpered and shook as she absorbed what I was saying.

Her long legs swung wide apart and she stretched out, then she pushed her legs out more and pointed and rotated her elegant feet and footwear.

Immediately, I pulled up the hem of her skirt and looked at her.

Sophie's legs were indeed long and beautiful. Her grey elasticised stockings clasped the top of her legs, and above her stockings I saw that she had left her knicker off, probably on Mary's advice, and I stared at the mass of small shiny black curls all around her vagina and up and over her *mons veneris*.

"You are beautiful, Sophie," I murmured, lifting my head and kissing her lips. And when I put my hand out and touched her, lightly running my fingers up her stockings and between her legs, she let out a girly squeal of delight.

"Oh yes, Helen, please touch me! Touch me! Oh yes, Helen! Do anything you like, Anything! Please!"

I reached around and unzipped her skirt, then dragged it roughly down over her legs. Then I dropped onto my knees, put a hand around each ankle and lifted her legs and dragged her closer to the edge of the bed. Then I buried my mouth into that mass of curls in search of her lips and her clitoris, and when I found her surprisingly large soft happy cherry thing, I sucked it and felt her shaking body and her crying, and knew that she was mine.

After a while, I sat up. Sophie stared at me and smiled, then her lips made puckering motions, wanting to be kissed, and her tongue disappeared into my mouth. Sophie would not let my head go, and we kissed and tongued until we both ran out of breath.

"Helen darling?"

"Yes, Sophie?"

'Take off your clothes for me, please Helen. I so want to see you.

"Yes, darling, I will, and I love it that you ask for the things you want."

As Sophie watched, I slipped my frock off over my head, leaving me in my suspenders and stockings, and shoes.

Sophie stared at me, appreciation showing on her face.

"My God, Helen, you are so beautiful."

"Thank you darling. I do love complements," I giggled.

I got up on the bed and straddled Sophie, and backed up to her face. Her hands grabbed me by the hips and in moments she was ravishing my pussy with her mouth. I shuddered and felt my vagina getting extremely wet.

Then I lay down on Sophie so that I could reach her pussy, and we quietly licked and sucked each other for a long time, sometimes having little orgasms along the way, and occasionally Sophie would squeal and shout my name or just a "Yes," or "More please."

Then I turned and went to her, and we put our arms around each other and kissed, and then kissed some more. And then we rested.

I asked Sophie to close her eyes, then I stretched my arm down, felt under the bed and retrieved the strap-on dildo. Then I held it close to her face and told her she could open her eyes and look at the present I had for her. She was at first shocked and then very impressed with it.

"I wish Adele could see this," Sophie laughed.

"Is Adele your girlfriend back home?" I ventured to ask.

"Was, sort of. She lives on a farm about half an hour's drive away. I used to take the ute and go and see her once a month when her folks were away at the big market. Adele never goes to town to the market. She's a big girl, fat I suppose you'd say, and not very good-looking and she can't stand people looking at her. She thinks the whole world is laughing at her."

"That is really sad, Sophie. Surely there is a man for her somewhere?"

"I reckon not. She's never gonna change. It is sad."

"You live a long way from everything too, don't you? You must both get very lonely. Have you ever thought of being lovers?"

Sophie rolled over and looked at me, then leant closer and kissed me.

"Almost, I suppose. I let her lick me a couple of times, a year or so ago, and I gave her pussy an occasional rub and she did the same to me. But we stopped doing it."

I was intrigued. This was an insight into the extremely lonely life of isolated Australian bush communities. These were young women who lived without access to other people, to anyone with whom they might find love.

"Oh, Sophie. I can't bear to think of someone like you living without love. Did the two of you ever talk about what you might do to change things?"

"Sadly, not. Adele has just given up on life. I guess if she lived in the city she'd probably be a drug addict. As it is, she's addicted to Kenny."

"Kenny? I thought you said there were no males around?"

Sophie laughed.

"Sorry Helen, Kenny is Adele's dog. A Golden Retriever. She spends all her time bathing it combing it and kissing it. She lets ..."

"She lets Kenny what?"

"She gets Kenny to do her."

"I'm sorry, sweetheart, I didn't get what you said?"

"Adele gets Kenny to shag her. She loves it. And Kenny doesn't seem to mind."

I turned and got up on my elbow.

"Sophie! You are not making sense, darling. People don't fuck their dogs. You're spinning me a yarn and I'm not happy with this story."

"Gee Helen. I am so sorry. What I'm telling you is true though. I've seen them do it. Adele invited me out to a little room behind the barn that she's decorated and it includes a low bed. I thought she was just going to show me her room, but it was more than that. I saw it all happen there. Then she wanted to share Kenny with me. That's when I stopped visiting her."

I was not handling this information very well. Bizarre acts between people I could sort of handle, but sex with animals? That was too difficult.

"Sophie! I think this conversation is doing my head in. We better stop it. Tell me a happy story, please."

There was silence for quite a while. In the end, I thought I'd spoken a bit harshly to Sophie, so I moved closer to her and held her hand.

"Sorry, Sophie. I hate to think of you in such unloving circumstances. I just want you to be here with me and Mary, safe, and feeling loved.

"And I want you to tell me you will stay and live here next door to me. And one other thing, wrap that bloody strap-on around your waist and make love to me, please. And kiss me, Sophie. I want your lips right now."

Sophie took a sharp inward breath and moved swiftly, first with a long loving kiss, then she kissed my clit, and then she worked out how to put on the strap-on.

I directed her to the bottle of lubricant and she gingerly wiped some on me. Then she held and inspected her new piece of equipment, laughingly pointing out that she was a "dildo virgin", and hoped I would be gentle with her.

We both laughed and I pulled her head back down and kissed her again.

"I have loved the short time we've had together, Helen. Thought I should say that right now, just in case I get it all wrong and you throw me out in the next few minutes."

"Darling Sophie! All you need do is slide it in. What you do then does not much matter, just so long as you do it with love. Even if you get a little carried away, I will know that you still love me. Pop it in, darling."

Being shagged by my loving new novice was wonderful. I asked her to hold my legs up straight so that I could look at them and include them in my "legs to the sky" fantasy. She did that and said how super cool it was, and that she had never ever been this excited about anything. And then she kissed me behind the knees and touched my feet, and kissed and licked my thighs above my stocking tops.

She was a natural with the dildo, not too hot, not too cold, but just right. And I could see that she loved doing it to me. Sophie's face was alive and happy, reaching around my back to pull my buttocks up towards her. And when I came suddenly, she screamed and came with me, and suddenly Sophie was laughing and crying at the same time.

Then I unbuckled her and attached the magic rubber cock around my waist. Then I turned her over and made her get on her knees, lubricated her and whispered, "This is your reward for giving me such a wonderful shagging."

She screamed in a mixture of anticipation and fear, as I inserted it. I didn't really know what life experience's she'd had and I wondered if the dildo was too big. But it slid in easily and she straight-away settled down to a regular rhythm and was soon calling out words of endearment and encouragement as we went.

I rolled her over so that I could lift her legs up and satisfy my visual lust. She moaned as I lifted them and moaned again when I told her to open her eyes and see how beautiful she looked and how she had the most beautiful legs in the world.

"Oh Helen, I so love what you are doing to me. Please keep going."

I lay between Sophie's legs and shagged the beautiful girl some more, unable to stop myself. But when I slowed, thinking it might be time to stop, she announced in a clear but quiet voice that she would like "some more, please". And when I suddenly began to thrash about and pushing right up into her to test her limits, she screamed out "Yes, Helen, yes, Helen, please Helen, keep doing it to me, Helen!" before she screamed a final "Yes", and exploded in an almighty orgasm which echoed through her body, and mine, for the next five minutes.

We fell into each other's arms and I covered us with the quilt.

"Helen?"

"Yes, my darling?"

"I will definitely stay and live with Auntie. I'm in love with you."

We pulled each other close and kissed; then exhausted, we fell asleep.

A week or so after she had spent time with Sophie instead of Mary, Helen thought about her upcoming meeting with Mary and realised that there was something she wanted to do with Mary, which she believed could benefit all her lovers.

She telephoned Mary.

"Hi Mary! It's me. No, I'm not ringing to cancel. Of course I want to see you, you silly thing. No! What I wanted to do was to put you on notice that I've decided to ask you to do something different tomorrow, but I'm too embarrassed to tell you what it is. We've never discussed it before. No, I can't tell you now either. Just wanted you to be forewarned that your lady lover might be kinkier than you thought. That's all. No! I'm not giving you a clue. No! I'm hanging up. Love you and see you tomorrow."

Helen smiled inwardly and thought how her loving husband Freddy might well get a present out of this, if it all worked out.

Mary was already at the studio when Helen got there. They both kissed and embraced each other.

"Are you going to tell me what this special thing is, or do I have to chase you around the room with your little flagellator up there on the wall. It's 'tell Mary' time."

Helen hugged and squeezed her large lover and sat her down beside her on the bed.

"Well, it's like this, Mary. There is something I like done to me that I find particularly exciting. My darling Freddy understands and happily gives it to me pretty regularly, and that is wonderful, but I'm a bit greedy and I would like to have more of it. I haven't known how to ask you for it, Mary, fearing you might think badly of me."

Mary stared at Helen wide-eyed, all the while clutching Helen's hands.

"Darling, what is it you want from me? You know I'll do anything you ask."

Helen took a deep breath.

"I want you to bugger me, Mary. Shag my bottom. I've bought a smaller strap on dildo designed just for that purpose. Anal sex is something I crave, Mary. There! I've said it."

Mary's jaw dropped. She was speechless. What Helen had just said was taking her a few moments to process.

"Say something Mary. Put me out of my misery."

"Helen. This might surprise you and I've never told anyone until now, but I've always wanted to try it but never knew how to go about getting started.

"A woman where I worked before I was married talked about it one day. She was very good-looking and looking back now, I think I probably had a crush on her but didn't know it. We lived quite close to each other and would catch the bus home together.

"Linda was her name. She told me that her new boyfriend was giving it to her every which way and when I asked her how many ways there were, she laughed and pointed to her mouth, between her legs and then, half turning, she pointed to her bum.

"When I asked which one she enjoyed the most, she giggled and pointed down behind her. Ever since that moment I've wondered about it and longed for a chance to try it, but the opportunity has never arisen.

"Helen, after all these years you might make that wish come true. If I work out how to do it to you, Helen, would you please be so good as to try and do it to me afterwards? I'll try not to make a fuss and if it's not for me at least I'll know I've had a try."

Now it was Helen who was speechless. Mary's answer had been totally unexpected.

"I am so surprised, Mary. I never dreamt that you even suspected that people did such things. I misjudged you entirely. You have made me so happy, I feel like crying. My dear Mary is going to liberate us both. I'm so excited."

Mary looked at Helen lovingly. "Tell me what we do next, Helen. I'm ready when you are."

Helen laughed. "I guess we simply do our usual loving sexy things, darling. Once we are warmed up, I will open up my back door for you and, hopefully my bottom will seduce you and revel in your loving attention."

"Oh, Helen? You make it sound sexy just by talking about it."

Mary fell backwards onto the bed, dragging Helen on top of her. Then she ran her hand down Helen's back and pulled her skirt up. She slid her hand into Helen's panties and ran her fingers down the crack of her bottom, lightly touching and resting on her tiny wrinkled orifice murmuring, "you are going to be mine, all mine."

Helen giggled. "Oh Mary. You are a dream come true."

Helen interrupted their passionate kissing and grinding of each other's bodies against each other and announced to Mary that she was ready.

Then she reached under a pillow and handed Mary a bottle of lubricating oil. From the drawer beside the bed she produced a small pink strap-on dildo. She licked the end of it provocatively as Mary watched. Then Mary took hold of it as Helen was still mouthing it and moved it gently in and out of Helen's mouth before taking it and putting it in her own mouth.

Helen smiled lovingly at Mary with that special pleading come-hither look as she watched Mary attached the dildo to her waist. Helen then rolled over, and pushed herself up onto her knees, pushed her bottom upwards, swaying slowly from side to side.

"I'm ready, my love. Come and bugger your lover. I want to feel you heaving up and down on my bottom, you sexy bitch. Please pour in some lube and get your legs between mine, right now."

In seconds, Mary had squeezed lubricant into Helen's anus and onto the dildo. Then she slipped in a finger and wriggled it about.

"Oh, Helen? This is so exciting."

Mary positioned herself between her lover's beautiful legs up close to her now wet perfumed rear and gently slid the slippery dildo into her pink, glistening and pulsating love hole.

"Yes, Mary! Yes, you darling! I can feel it and it is wonderful. Shag me my sweet. I might make a noise and call you names as you get going but don't worry. It's because I'm in heaven."

Mary groaned appreciatively. "I'm already calling you a randy bitch, Helen. And I couldn't be more randy myself."

"Just fuck me, you big beautiful slut. Give it to me now, hard. Oh! Oh! Yes, you are such a slut, Mary. You've never had me like this before, have you, you slut? You are very naughty. This poor bottom will never be safe from you again. You will want it again won't you Mary. You do like it, don't you sweetheart. Say you like it."

Mary's heaving buttocks increased momentum.

"Yes, I love it. I've orgasmed once already just from starting to fuck you, you dirty little whore. How could I not want to push you over and get into your bum? Of course I will want to do this; for ever, Helen."

Helen was now making gurgling noises as she murmured "Yes, Yes, Oh yes! Harder you beautiful bitch. Oh yes, Mary! You can fuck me like this any time you want to. Oh my God! You feel so good, you sleazy slut. I love you, you randy bum-fucker. Just don't stop. Don't stop. I'm coming, I'm coming. Yes, Yes, Aah!"

Helen and Mary lay side by side holding hands and catching their breath after their lengthy first anal session.

"You are so good at this, Mary."

The two women laughed.

"I must have a natural talent then, Helen. I hope it works both ways. I'm a little bit nervous about my first lesson. You must be patient with me, darling. Can old bitches learn new tricks? You know what they say."

They both laughed. Then Helen slid her hand under her lover's very large backside and touched her bottom hole with an oily finger. Then she gently slid it in and slowly moved it about.

"You will be fine, darling. And if you don't like it the first time, we can always try little sessions occasionally, just for my sake. My thrills come first of course, you naughty girl."

On Helen's instructions, Mary rolled over and got up onto her knees. Helen slipped a fresh condom onto the dildo and strapped it on and positioned herself between Mary's legs, surveying her lover's magnificent backside. Then with a hand on each buttock, she moved them apart so that she could see her target. She dribbled oil on to Mary's anus and then slipped in an index finger. Mary gave a little start and took a sharp intake of breath in anticipation of what was to follow.

Helen moved her finger slowly round and round in Mary's bottom and then, when there had been no suggestion of discomfort from Mary, she oiled the dildo and slipped the first inch or two into the place for which it was intended. Then she pushed it in further and began to move backwards and forwards.

Helen loved the feeling of Mary's soft buttock cheeks flapping against the lower part of her belly and the wet, smelly pussy hair of both women rubbing together reminded her of the intense orgasm she had experienced when Mary pushed in hard in those last moments.

"I'm going to push it right in now, Mary. Hope you're comfortable with that my darling?"

"Very comfortable," came the reply.

"And then I'm going to shag you good and proper, you voluptuous whore."

"Be my guest, slut slave. I'm loving it so far. Don't hold back Helen. I'm into it already. It feels great. I'm just waiting for my arse-fucking slut to get into it properly and stop worrying about me."

Helen slapped a buttock to let Mary know who was boss.

"Oh! Oh! Yes, all right! I'm ready for anything. Forget about me. Just do what you want with that pink prick thingy."

Helen began a serious shagging of Mary's delightful backside, and as she did so the idea ran through her head that, if Mary really did enjoy this, it would be a wonderful present for both Freddy and Mary should the opportunity arise.

Helen experimented. Sometimes she climbed up higher and pushed downwards and at other times she moved down and pushed up. Mary seemed to respond more excitedly when Helen pushed down and Helen settled on that as their preferred movement.

Helen was now forgetting about Mary, concentrating instead on her own needs. She started by biting Mary's shoulders. Then she slid a hand underneath the two of them and fondled Mary's pussy. "Oh God! Yes, please my love!" Mary gasped.

It was not long before Mary screamed.

"Oh God! Yes, Yes, Yes!"

Then Helen joined in Mary's orgasm with a giant one of her own.

Mary buckled and lay on her stomach. But Helen wasn't finished yet.

"No, slut. You can't get away that easily".

Now that Mary was lying flat, she changed hands on Mary's clit and spread the fingers on her other hand around the back of Mary's neck and squeezed it tight, pushing her face down forcefully into the bed. At the same time, she pushed the pink prick especially hard into Mary's arse. Mary screamed.

"You fucking slut? Oh, God, Yes, Yes! Oh God! Yes, my bum and pussy belong to you, Helen. Oh my God! Fuck me, fuck me, oh yes. You're fucking me silly, Helen."

Helen fell to one side, pulled Mary's face around to hers and pushed her tongue into Mary's mouth, wildly rubbing her own clitoris at the same time. Then Helen screamed "Mary! Yes!" as she came, pulling Mary on top of her. They pushed their saturated pussies against each other and both women came again amid screams of passion and delight.

For these two lovers, bottom play was now firmly on the agenda.

Mary awoke to different world. She felt different. Hungry! At first she thought she was simply hungry for food but then she had another thought. She wasn't hungry for food, Mary wanted something else, something she could touch and feel. Mary wanted to feel another body. And the feeling was really intense.

Mary touched herself, her breasts her thighs, her sex. Then she thought about her new medication. Her doctor had prescribed a course of hormone replacement therapy when Mary went to her a week ago and said that she was feeling a bit run down and out of sorts.

Doctor Meg had smiled and written a prescription and told her to get straight back to her if Mary thought that the dosage was not right.

It wasn't as though the world had really changed. Yes, Sophie was pregnant and this was now a factor in their relationship. The two women were still lovers but less often did they roll around in the bed together. They were indeed now living like an older married couple. Both women were handling it quite well. Neither complained about not getting what they used to have and they both still cared very much for each other.

Mary was also aware that things had change for Sophie since her encounter with Frederico in Helen's studio when Freddy was on his way home from giving Mary her sexy birthday present.

From being a twenty something year old woman who had never been with a man, Sophie was now carrying Freddy's baby from that one chance accidental hook-up and now Mary sensed that Sophie was in love with Freddie and thought about him constantly.

Mary wondered if Helen realised how deeply Sophie was in love with Freddy and did Freya also know how Sophie felt about the man who was also fathering her future child. Did Freya also carry these loving feelings for Freddy? Had Helen omitted to consider the emotional consequences of what had happened?

All this was vitally important but in the short term, Mary's day to day emotional and physical needs were rising up and likely to take over.

Mary feeling so horny was now a thing she could no longer ignore.

Other things had changed recently, too, although in this instance Mary regarded it as a positive rather than a negative. Her long time friend Janice was now permanently employed at a a nursing home and so the timing of their usual morning coffee and their loving romp on the bed had necessarily moved to a different day. But it wasn't just the timing that had changed. Janice's new job had made her a different person in the bedroom. She was no longer simply the compliant receiver of Mary's lustful advances. Janice now asserted her self in many different ways, bringing home her experiences with her lesbian boss and her many adoring nursing aids.

Janice brought unwashed stockings, still bearing the perfume of her little nursing aids creaming on her legs, and rubbed them against Mary's face while recounting in vivid detail how she made the girls cum on her.

Everyone knew her as Sister Janice and thought she had been a nun and this ruse had been the reason for many of her sexual encounters.

Mary was now also the recipient of a number of semi-violent manoeuvres that Janice brought from her encounters with her boss. Janice tied Mary up with silk chords and plugged both of Mary's orifices at the same time as she whipped her with a small flagellator. Mary screamed and threw herself about but when it was all over, she melted into Janice's arms, sucking the woman's tiny breasts while sobbing happily while her genitals still throbbed as she enjoyed the aftermath.

Mary made changes too. Janice had always refused to try anal sex, but now that she was experiencing more erotic experiences, she found herself encouraging Mary who was now at last able to let herself go mad on and in her lovers magnificent bubble-butt derriere.

"Oh, Janice, you beautiful slut. I want to ride you like this forever."

"Ride me like this for as long as you like Mary. I'm converted and I want more. Fuck my arse hard you big bitch."

Janice and Mary now seemed closer than they had ever been and over cups of tea and coffee, Janice told how her subterfuge as an innocent nun had begun when she was at Mary's birthday party and jokingly suggested it to Maria and Serina who were both most attentive. Going home with the two women and having a sexual fantasy moment with the hot mother and daughter, pretending she was one of their naughty convent school nuns led eventually to Janice getting the job at the old priests' home.

Mary swore to keep this information secret, especially as she was now the beneficiary of Janice's ever expanding sex life.

So what was this hunger? Mary had her suspicions. It wasn't just the new medication but rather the new more passionate and daring responses she and Janice were exploring. Mary's sexual emotions where being slowly drawn towards a more animal lust where anticipation and not knowing what would happen next, could cause excitement. Mary wanted surprises in her sex life.

———————

Maude had hired Mary to look after the daily running of the music school premises for the four days that she was going to be away. There wasn't a lot to do other than make sure that the current nine residents' coming and going went smoothly. Someone needed to be there in case of an emergency. Plus there were occasional inquiries by phone or mail to which Mary would respond with a mailing piece and friendly conversation or simply provide information by email.

There was also a new person checking in. Carmela Russo was a young singer from Griffith in central New South Wales. She would be delivered by a friend sometime tomorrow, most likely in the early afternoon. Carmela was training to sing opera and was already a well known teenage performer in her Italian community back home in that now famous fruit growing region south-west of the Blue Mountains.

———————

Mary wandered into the shady hallway of number nineteen. She thought she was alone but then the door of Unit One opened and the friendly face of Maria appeared.

"Hi, Mary. Just finishing up before I head off to another job. I'll be away only a couple of hours then I'll come back here. Grandpa Aldo and his friend Giorgio are working in Maude's garden today so I need to keep an eye on them. Italy is going soccer crazy at the moment because of the European cup. The Juventus versus Real Madrid match is all the men talk about. I just need to make sure that they work as well as talk football.

"Mary, you look a bit down. Are you okay?"

While Mary knew Maria and Serina quite well, they had never had intimate conversations. There was no reason. It just hadn't happened. Mary only recently became aware from a conversation with Janice that

there was more to the two women than she had ever imagined, inter-
estingly, in a sexual context.

"I've just started hormone replacement therapy, Maria, and I'm not
sure whether or not the dosage is right. I feel a little bit agitated,
Maria, or more truthfully I should say that I feel decidedly horny."

Maria's smiling face looked at Mary intently.

"That is interesting Mary. Damn! I forgot to water Maude's potted
palm. Follow me in here for a moment Mary while I fix it."

The two women moved back into the room and Maria filled a
watering can from the bathroom. Then on the way back she went up
to Mary and put her face close to Mary's.

"More often than not, these things can have a simple solution,
Mary."

She continued staring intently at Mary then turned slowly and
moved over towards the potted plant.

"I find that when I feel like you are feeling Mary, I make myself
reach out for what I want."

Mary listened as she watched Maria bending over in front of her to
water the plant, noticing the woman's neat and shapely figure.

"I think if you see something that grabs your attention and you
know that you want it then its best to just take it while you can,
Mary."

Maria placed the watering can down on the carpet and while still
bent over, took hold of the hem of her skirt and lifted it up and back
to display her perfect bottom to Mary.

"You are more than welcome to put your hands anywhere you
want Mary. I know I would love it. I'm horny most of the time dear
lady so you can please me as well as yourself."

Mary gasped and she stared at the vision in front of her. Maria's
backside was beautiful. Without a second thought, Mary moved
forward and placed both hands on the waiting woman.

"Oh, Maria, you are such a darling. Oh, my God, yes. This is
exactly what I need." The feeling of Maria's naked bottom on the
palms of her hands was electrifying.

Maria wriggled and rotated her bottom slowly in a show of appreciation while Mary fondled and groped her

"I will have to leave you in a few minutes darling. But I will come back with more if you would like me to, or maybe to your house later?"

Mary was rubbing Maria's beautiful posterior and licking her shiny firm buttocks.

"Mary?"

"Yes, Maria?"

"Just quickly, please pull down your knickers and rub yourself against me. Then finger me between my legs. That will keep me wet for a while."

All too soon the woman were forced to stop so that they could get on with their duties

"Now Mary, there is something I should warn you about regarding our soccer crazed gardeners."

"Warn me about? What do I need to worry about, Maria."

"I suspect it's only a Sicilian thing but I should tell you in case something happens while I'm away. Those two reprobates in the garden are great fun and the truth is Mary, I let each of them get between my legs, quite often, as does Serena. They both have magnificent cocks."

Mary stared at the beautiful woman in awe.

"Maria? I'm shocked and intrigued? Tell me more."

"Well, you being a new female wandering about coupled with them both being so excited about the match, well, they are likely to open their pants and display their cocks."

"Good heavens, Marie, what do I need to do?"

Maria eyed Mary with amusement.

"It is up to you darling woman. Respond as you feel the need. Maybe as you did to me a moment ago? They are both rough diamonds but they have good hearts and would never hurt anyone. Now I must go. Best of luck if it happens.

"One last thought. Before we had our moment together just now, I was considering leading Giorgio down between the runner beans and the snow peas when I got back this afternoon. That way I could have him doggy style while I was happily eating fresh peas. I can usually get at least four orgasms out of Giorgio before he comes. By the way,

Giorgio prefers pussy where grandpa has a penchant for both pussy and a willing arse."

Maria reached out and pulled Mary close to her, slipping her hand into Mary's pants for a final tiny loving squeeze.

"Stay moist, Mary. For a woman, it's the answer to all of life's problems."

Mary stood and watched Maria disappear through the door while noting that the longing in her excited pussy was demanding her attention. Mary moved towards Maude's bed and fell back. With firm stroking while reviewing images of Maria's beautiful rear end in her mind's eye, she came and the release was sublime. And moments later, she was thinking of those gardeners who she might meet later in the day.

Maria's advice urging Mary to stay moist might not be a problem after all.

Mary was suddenly brought back to the present when the phone rang in the office. It was a wrong number but the interruption served to bring her focus back to her administrative duties, and for a while she was able to forget about her hormones and her symptoms.

The diary said that the accountant, Giovanni Romano would be calling in early in the afternoon to go through the monthly accounts. Mary had already met this handsome man who was purportedly a singer of opera and she thought how he seemed like a thorough gentleman.

Mary busied herself with catching up with the filing of correspondence, something Maude avoided on the pretence she would need to look at a letter again soon. Then Mary printed out mailing labels in readiness for next months newsletter posting.

In between times, Mary made a cup of tea and ate the slice of fruit cake she'd brought from home.

At noon, Mary took her sandwich and went out into the garden to sit in the old summerhouse near the vegetable garden, and enjoy the sun, her summer dress moving in the light summer breeze.

As Mary moved down the garden path and came nearer to the summerhouse, the sound of mens voices calling out reminded Mary of Maria's warning. Was this Giorgio and Aldo carrying on about the World Cup? And what had Maria said they might do? Surely she was making those things up. Mary smiled at the thought of the two men being as outrageous as Maria suggested they might be. Then Mary turned the corner and saw that it was true. Both men were sitting on the summerhouse steps happily eating their sandwiches and drinking their vino; and yes, the two mens' trousers were open, and yes, two cocks stood at half-mast.

A radio played quietly close by and Mary heard the roar of a crowd and cheering. Then grandpa Aldo and Giorgio spotted Mary and called out and beckoned her to come and join them. The men were excited by the soccer match and even more so when they realised they had company.

Aldo patted the step in between the two men and invited Mary to join them, smiling and calling out 'Juventus' and 'Italia'.

Maria felt a little apprehensive as she seated herself between the two men, but she was feeling something else as well, something akin to her recent hunger feelings.

She tried not looking at the mens genitals and pretended she hadn't noticed them. Grandpa Aldo poured Mary a beaker of wine and passed it to her, speaking to her softly in Italian but finishing with her name in English. He remembered her name from the time he met her at the house warming party Maude had given more than a month ago.

Mary remembered that Aldo had overtly ogled her, putting his hand on her rear and moving her around, obviously impressed with her backside.

Mary turned and looked at Giorgio, nodding and smiling and acknowledging his presence. The two men then continued what seemed like an ongoing conversation about the football match.

Mary sat back and got comfortable, happy that they were relaxed enough in her presence to continue simply talking to each other, and probably much as they had been doing before she'd arrived.

While the two men carried on, Mary observed each of them out the corners of her eyes. Was what Maria said, true. Did she really let these men have her?

Mary could see the attraction. The simple manliness of the two characters was a lot different to most of the men Mary knew. They seemed so self-assured and comfortable in their honest interactions with their world. But then Mary was alerted to something that was happening and she felt a moment of panic.

Aldo had put a hand on Mary's thigh and moments later, Giorgio put his hand on her other thigh. She glanced at the faces of the two men, both of whom were happily smiling at her. Then Mary glanced down and got a bigger shock. Both mens cocks had grown to be very large and stood tall between their legs and if that wasn't surprising enough, when each man took one of Mary's hands and wrapped her fingers around their erections, Mary experienced a moment of grave fear mixed with a strange counter emotion of excitement.

When the men let go of Mary's hands, they watched her face to see her reaction. She looked from one to the other, stoney faced, not knowing what she should do. But then something happened. Mary suddenly felt a wetness in her vagina and she heard Maria's final words from earlier in the day, "Stay moist, Mary. For a woman, it's the answer to all of life's problems."

Mary offered the men just a hint of a smile, but then she tightened her grip on their cocks and their already happy smiles broadened.

Aldo lent across and lifted the hem of Mary's frock, pulling it back so that her large thighs were adequately displayed

The two men continued their animated conversations about soccer, leaving Mary alone with her thoughts and her feelings. She loved it that their cocks felt welcoming to her touch and loved the excitement her body felt when one cock or the other pulsated or throbbed in response to Mary moving her hands.

Mary's hunger was being nourished in a way she would never have expected. Womanly erotic feelings floated joyously to the fore and Mary fantasised unabashedly about what she had in her hands. She began to gently move her hands up and down on each penis, relishing the feeling and intrigued at each ones ability to grow even bigger and harder.

Sitting like this in the sun with her eyes closed and happily holding on to two manhoods was beginning to have an effect on Mary. Loving things as they were was fine, but having got to this point, what should she think about doing next. Could she suck each of them in turn? Would they want to fuck her as a result?

That decision was made for her by what happened next.

"Can I join you?" A deep gentle male voice came from just in front of Mary, startling her and she opened her eyes.

"Mr Romano! I wasn't expecting you for a while yet. These two are celebrating the soccer. I'm sure they would love to include you too,"

Mary was confused. She knew she should have let go of the two men but the unexpected suddenness of Mr Romano's arrival made that seem pointless. Perhaps he would understand how the celebrations were progressing, him being Italian as well.

"Call me Giovanni, Mary. It's you I would like to join."

Mary stared and watched totally dumfounded as Mr Romano unzipped his trousers and dropped them around his knees. Then he pushed down his boxer shorts and produced something extraordinary.

Set amid more pubic hair than she ever imagined anyone having, an already large penis was stretching up and expanding rapidly and what's more, it was pointed directly at Mary.

Aldo and Giorgio laughed and yelled appreciatively, and Mary gasped.

Giovanni stepped closer so that the head of his now enormous cock waved gently in front of Mary's mouth.

"Open your mouth, Mary. This is for you."

The gentlemanly Giovanni reached forward and put a hand behind Mary's head and slowly moved it towards him.

Mary couldn't refuse. His cock was beautiful and like nothing she'd ever seen before. She first licked the head of it and then she began to take it into her mouth. It was so big and hard that she wondered whether she would be able to manage it. But then Giovanni held back a little, happy to just rock his cock backwards and forwards in between Mary's lips and her teeth.

Mary became aware of something else happening. Aldo was reaching his hand up between her legs and she felt two large rough fingers slide into her very wet cunt. Mary's glazed eyes tried to focus but the feelings in her cunt and in her mouth were so wonderful, she didn't want to think about anything more. Everything was so very wonderful. Mary's hunger was being properly fed at last.

Mary had no idea how long she had been enjoying herself, but suddenly, a woman's voice invaded Mary's revelry.

"You lucky slut, Mary. I'm so happy that you found a way to keep wet."

Mary opened her eyes and looked at the beaming Maria.

Maria looked up at Giovanni and smiled, "Beautiful cock Mr Romano. I can see why Maude likes it so much. Make sure it does the right thing by my friend Mary. She deserves a proper shagging. And maybe you'd like to try me one day? Or Mary and I can arrange a double act if you're interested."

The energetic Maria smiled at Mary and leant and kissed her on the forehead.

"Just came to take Giorgio for a ride in the vegetable patch."

Maria removed Mary's hand that was still attached to Giorgio's cock and wrapped her own fingers around it.

"Come along dearest man. Let me take you for a walk. Avanti! Venire!"

When Maria spoke to him in Italian he quickly rose and followed the amazing woman around the corner to fulfil his obligations.

After Maria and Giorgio had left, it wasn't long before Aldo and Giovanni lifted Mary up off the step and moved her onto the carpet inside the summerhouse. The two men removed her dress and her bra and pants and then commenced a most serious shagging threesome and one that Mary would never forget.

First Giovanni laid her on her back and held up her legs and fed his enormous cock into her welcoming cunt. Then after shagging her to orgasm, he let Aldo have his way.

Giovanni laid on his back and Aldo helped Mary to first kneel and then to climb on top of Giovanni, feeding the man's cock back into her. When that was accomplished, Aldo moved up behind Mary and placed his cock between her large buttocks and it was only moments before Mary had enthusiastically opened her back door to him and welcomed Aldo to the party.

All three lovers rhythmically danced a sexual ritual that had been played out over the centuries. Two men and a woman embedded in a heavenly tryst. What more could Mary want.

Maria called on Mary one afternoon after Maria had finished work. She had phoned ahead and said that she had things to tell Mary which she thought might interest her.

After Mary had made love to Aldo and Giovanni the week before, instead of being more settled in herself, her sexual hunger had increased and she was wanting even more sex. Mary expressed these thoughts to Maria when they ran into each other at the local shopping centre.

"I just don't understand," Mary told Maria on the telephone. "The doctor assures me that the medication I'm taking is fine. So I've no idea why I'm in what seems like a permanent state of lust."

When Maria arrived at the house, she quickly assured Mary that she wasn't bringing bad news and that there was nothing wrong and that her visit was about things which were good and might help Mary.

"There are women like us, Mary, who just need to make love more often. Actually, I would put the number like us at around seventy-percent of women except many don't know and will probably never know what ails them.

"Staying healthy and happy demands that we live our lives fully and without too many restraints. I'm here because I believe I can offer you a solution, an answer to a horny woman's every fantasy."

Mary giggled and topped up Maria's coffee cup.

"Forgive me, Maria but you do sound as though you've taken on the local Tuppaware agency. Should I be worried?"

Maria laughed. "Now that you mention it, I do, don't I? But no, I'm here to tell you a story and you can tell me when I've finished, what you think. It will take a little while to tell, so please bear with me. But do interrupt at any time if you have a question.

Without saying where it was, Maria began to tell Mary about The Club.

"Imagine a place that is super safe, clean and well run and comfortable, where women can go to interact with men or women in order to enjoy a wide range of mutually agreed upon sexual exploits. I'm here to tell you that there is now such a place and I want to tell you about it.

Over the next forty minutes, Maria provided details of the organisation of The Club and the required code of behaviour. She thought it best to begin with what happens at the club because that was really what people want to know most and what Mary would be most interested in asking questions about.

And ask questions, she did.

By the time Maria had completed her discourse, Mary was truly excited. Maria asked her to repeat some of the things she'd said just to be sure that she had understood the main points.

"So, Maria. I go to The Club and I'm wanting to meet a man, or as you've pointed out, maybe more than one man. I find a seat anywhere in rows six or seven, and settle back to watch the movie.

After just a short wait, a man will come and sit beside me and after a few minutes he will attempt to touch me, most likely on a leg or a breast or an arm. Then its up to me how I respond, encouraging him or discouraging him. If you want to make him work for his grope, refuse him a couple of times, three max, otherwise he will assume your not up for it. To get of rid of him, four rebuttals should do or just keep moving his hand away.

Meanwhile a second or even a third man might turn up and suddenly I've got more than I can safely handle."

Maria laughed at Mary's childlike enthusiasm.

"You've got it Mary."

"If I'm not getting any takers in six or seven, I can go and pick a shy bloke from rows four or five and do whatever I like with him.

"And if I want to meet up with a woman, I go and sit in rows eight and nine. In those rows we approach each other with signals - smiles and hand gestures. Sensitive touching and groping, and kissing and licking coming a few minutes later.

And if I'm with someone and we don't want to be interrupted by another horny person, we sit in rows ten, eleven or twelve. We also sit in those rows if we simply want to be alone and watch the movie and play with ourselves.

And finally, if I want to get ravaged, I go and park myself in row three where, in just a few moments I will be deluged with gropers and cock wavers prancing around in front and behind me.

The two woman laughed and Maria commented that she would love to make a movie of Mary on her first visits and how it could be hilarious.

"Now do you remember what other stuff is on offer, Mary?"

"Yep! Haven't forgotten a thing. The Gals Only room is where you can go with girlfriends to canoodle more comfortably, and you will also find dildo's there in two sizes. You can also have a wee and powder your nose. You can even use it as a bolt hole to escape from over zealous blokes.

"The Parlour is like the Gals Only room but it caters for both sex couples.

"Lastly, Home Deliveries sounds like the stand out! The sin-bin. Girls can make a booking and say how many blokes they would like to entertain. Allowable numbers are two, three and four."

"How am I doing, Maria, and where the bloody hell can I find this place?"

"Just tell me a couple of the rules Mary. I need to know that you know the rules."

"Easy, Maria, and number one, don't give anyone your name, phone number or address or any information that will allow them to find you anywhere other than at The Club.

"Arrive at The Club clean and properly clothed. I guess that means not covered in shit, and naked.

"Oh yes, important! Avoid getting into conversations. Talking is anathema to fulfilling your lustful desires. We all remember the visual hunk on sporting TV who made the mistake of trying to talk? And the same goes for women."

"So, my love. Just one more question. Would you like to come along as my guest next Tuesday afternoon. If you enjoy it, I'm allowed three visitor passes a year so that you can come with me again. So Mary? Are you game? Can you face all those horny men and women?"

Mary's face became very serious as she murmured, "Yes please Maria. I would love that."

Mary's had a lot of trouble accepting that The Club was within walking distance of her house. This seemed so ridiculous as to bring Maria's whole story into question. It wasn't until she was safely in the door and facing the wonderful Alvie, as she attached her visitor number, that Mary begin to think the story was true.

"There you go love. Come back and see me if you have any problems."

"I told you how I would be meeting a girlfriend here didn't I? Veronica and I have known each other for years and we work together sometimes. She and I usually sit in rows eight or nine, mainly to meet girls, but occasionally we hook up with a bloke or two. And if we are fishing for a man, we'll move back a couple of rows. You can sit with us while you're settling in and then wander off to explore and see the sights. You might be shocked."

Mary looked around, wide-eyed.

"It is so beautifully designed, isn't it."

"Wait until you've seen the cinema, Mary. That is the centre of this world."

Veronica called out as she arrived through the front door and the two waited for her to join them. Maria introduced them.

"I've already filled Veronica in on who you are Mary. She said she was excited for you and wished it was her first time. But that is what we always say about anything, isn't it."

The three entered the dimly lit cinema and Maria pointed out that Mary's eyes would soon adjust so that she would be able to see everything going on around her, to which Veronica responded with, "but she really only wants to see the hot bits, like the rest of us."

Tuesday was just another normal day at The Club and as with

every other day, activity hotted up a bit an hour or so after The Club opened.

Maria and Veronica stood each side of Mary and each took a hand so that she didn't fall down.

"A lot of people in heels topple over in the isles because of the steep slope and the dim lighting."

Mary suddenly found herself staring down at the movie screen watching as a woman attempted to swallow a very large penis while making sucking noises. She wanted to keep watching but her friends wanted to move her on.

"You said I could just come and sit in the front row and watch the movie, didn't you, Maria?"

"Yes, darling, but surely you wouldn't deny all the other people access to your delightful self. What a waste of a body that would be."

"She will probably never look at the screen again, once she gets active, don't you think, Veronica?"

Mary suddenly stopped in her tracks. "Oh my God, I've just noticed something."

Maria and Veronica laughed and Veronica said, "Well thank God for that. And do you like what you are seeing, Mary?"

Maria and Veronica smiled at each other in the dim light and glanced over to where Mary was staring. A few seats up and across the other side of the next isle, a woman was on her knees on her seat and a man behind her had just pulled down her panties and was feeling between her legs. In front of the woman, another man was holding out his erection towards her face as an offering.

Mary gazed at the scene in silence. She was mesmerised.

Maria noticed a woman heading slowly up towards the threesome.

"Mary? Just watch that woman approaching the people who you are looking at. She is coming towards them from the other side of the row. I think she's moving in to try and get some of the action."

Mary looked and gasped. "My God you're right. Look! She's got her hands on the cock of the man at the back and she's helping him put it into the lady without knickers. And look, another man is arriving and he's pulling up the dress of the woman who has just arrived. This is incredible."

Veronica giggled, "They must be early starters. There's not usually that much action until a bit later.

Maria agreed, "She is obviously a morning person."

"Welcome to The Club, Mary. Veronica and I hope you will enjoy yourself."

Maria and Veronica looked at each other and smiled. Then they moved as one, leading Mary to a seat in row seven and each took a seat on either side of her. Then Veronica turned and smiled at Mary and reached down and lifted Mary's skirt and stared excitedly at her substantial blue stockinged legs while Maria unbuttoned Mary's top, releasing her huge bust. Then Maria pulled down the bra straps and eased two big beautiful bosoms from their cups and rubbed her fingers on a nipple.

Veronica reached under Mary's backside and found the top of her knickers and slowly pulled them down and over her knees while Maria licked and kissed Mary's massive breasts.

Mary had initially made noises of protest, but not for long. She had wanted to watch the couple up further, but she realised that what she had here was much better.

Veronica began to kiss Mary on the lips while gently caressing her large bare thighs above her stockings and this quickly turned into a passionate exchange. Mary turned and embraced Veronica around the shoulders and wanted to completely devour the small woman. Veronica responded and took Mary's hand and guided it up under her short skirt and whispered to Mary, "Please feel me up, Mary. Finger me you beautiful woman."

This first time with the girls was getting Mary's juices running as they hadn't for a very long time. It suddenly reminded her of Helen's seduction of her the year before. It felt almost similarly religious which sounded silly. But having her hands busily discovering the small delicate woman's special places was amazing.

"Oh Veronica, you little darling. I just want to fuck your beautiful little pussy."

Maria likewise dragged Mary's other hand up under her skirt and pressed her fingers to her vagina. But then the women were suddenly interrupted.

Another woman joined them and was kissing Maria while removing her own top and exposing her bosom. Maria responded quickly, dragging the stranger's top off and then sucking her breasts. Moments later, a man arrived and touched both women's breasts while his erection stood waving in the air.

The newly arrived woman stopped and looked at it then took hold of it and sucked it briefly before looking around at everyone before asking if any of them needed a cock in their cunt.

To Mary's surprise, Veronica called out. "Yes please. Come around to this side and I'll have it, thanks."

Veronica turned and looked lovingly at Mary.

"You've made my pussy feel really good Mary so I'll have some cock to go with it. I can usually come in a very short time when I get fucked. You will enjoy it too, my love. I'll make sure of that.

The man made his way around to the other side and parked himself next to Veronica.

"Mary, darling. Will you give him a suck and a rub and make him wet while I position myself to climb onto him."

Mary did as she was asked, reaching her head down and taking hold of the gentleman's quite large cock. She lovingly tugged at it then she leant over and put her mouth over it and slurped saliva on him.

Moments later, Veronica lifted herself up and impaled the man's member in her tiny pussy. Then she jiggled up and down energetically and in no time, she gurgled and moaned and twitched and came. Then she removed him and suddenly she was back kissing Mary like she'd never left.

It all happened so quickly and Mary found that she had loved the whole event, so much so that she was now totally in love with the doll-like Veronica.

The man disappeared and then Mary heard Maria scream and looked down to see her thrusting her cunt hard agains the mouth of the unknown woman and it seemed that the woman was coming at the same time and just a few moments later the two were enjoying celebratory kissing. Mary heard Maria whisper, "Thank you", and the woman replying "my pleasure". Then the visitor was gone.

Maria reached across Mary and slipped a hand into Veronica's tiny bra.

"I love you two horny bitches. You are the best!"

If Mary thought the party was over, she was wrong.

"I need a pee," announced Veronica as she adjusted her clothing.

"I'm taking Mary to the Gals Room. We'll take a booth and relax. We so want to eat each other out, don't we my darling?" Veronica looked lovingly at Mary.

"Hope that's okay with you Maria. I'll catch you tomorrow if you're not here when we come out."

Maria looked at Mary and reached out and took her hand and smiled wickedly.

"You might be about to have the best moments of your visit, Mary. Just do whatever Veronica tells you and enjoy yourself."

Veronica led the way back up the aisle, walking slowly so that Mary could look around at what other folk were up to. Mary was still partly dazed from recent events plus she was excitedly attempting to foresee her upcoming moments with Veronica.

Mary was torn between staring at the beautiful apparition of Veronica's perfect little body swaying from side to side in front of her, and perving on the club members activities on either side.

For her benefit, Veronica would stop when she thought Mary might be interested to gaze on a particular exchange of sexual favours happening close by.

Each time she did this, she would kiss Mary on her cheek and fondle her buttocks and nod her head towards what she had noticed and while Mary watched with fascination as one woman helped another by dragging a cock she was sucking, over to perform in between her friends legs, Veronica continued to run a hand over Mary's posterior. And when Mary stared at a woman who was pretending to be oblivious to the fact that her naked breasts were being gently groped by a man sitting behind her, Veronica nibbled Mary's ear and whispered endearing messages, telling her what she wanted Mary to do to her once they were alone.

As the two neared the top of the aisle, Veronica stopped and nodded towards what was happening in the notorious row three, known to some as The Jungle and to others as Gang-bang Alley.

"This is where you come for something fast and furious, Mary. Maria occasionally likes to park herself there but I make her do it without me. I'm not against it and I would like to try it one day, but not yet. I think it's because I'm so small and I'm frightened it might be too rough. Besides, there are more than enough nice and more gentle things to do here."

Mary's mouth dropped and she whispered, "Oh my God!", staring at what was happening in row three.

Two near naked women were kneeling on their seats, side by side and with their rear ends thrust upwards and slowly wriggling to entice the half-a-dozen men who stood behind them taking turns filling their cunts and arses. The womens heads were resting on the backs of the seats and their mouths were being fed by a platoon of penises. As one cock was being sucked, the woman's hands would be tugging on two others.

Every so often one of the two women would scream loudly and it would rise above the hubbub of the cinema.

"I'd guess that those two are friends and they came here either as a dare or to celebrate something; a divorce maybe. Row three doesn't get a lot of visitors so your quite privileged to see this rare event."

Mary was dumfounded and deep down, she was sexually aroused by what she was watching.

Then Veronica turned Mary's head and kissed her.

"Come along darling. The Gals Room is just here. I want you."

While Veronica went into the toilet for a pee, Mary surveyed the Gals Only room. It was tastefully furnished with a low table, arm chairs and two sofa's. A huge vase of fresh flowers adorned the table and jugs of water and glasses sat on a side cupboard and etchings of erotic artworks hung on the walls. There were six doors which opened on to private booths and four were ajar and when Mary peeped into one, she could see that these too, had vases of flowers and water jugs and artworks on the walls as well as two armchairs and a bed on which lay pillows and bolsters.

Mary could hear happy giggles and squeals and moaning coming from the two booths where the doors were closed. One door showed a red engaged sign but the second showed green meaning it wasn't locked. The other difference was that the first had the curtains pulled completely across but the windows on the second occupied booth were only partly closed, allowing anyone to peep in.

Veronica later told Mary that partly drawn curtains and a green door sign signalled that the occupants would be happy to receive visitors.

Mary would have liked to peep but then Veronica re-appeared and took Mary's hand and led her to a booth and they went in. She locked the door and pulled across the curtains then turned and took Mary in her arms and reached up on her toes and the two kissed.

Both women were excited to be alone together and Mary nervously watched as Veronica dropped her skirt to the floor and stepped out of it, displaying her perfect little body. Mary stared at this most youthful looking fifty-something year-old and a part of her cried out, wanting to devour Veronica or even to be Veronica, standing there in her red stockings and suspender belt and red stilettos and her naughty little red bra that only just reached above her nipples. Veronica's straight black bobbed hair framed her beautiful face and accentuated the wide always open smiling mouth and big cupid lips and emphasised the tiny doll's big angelic brown eyes.

Veronica bent down and lifted the hem of Mary's dress, lifting it up and over her head and dropping it on a chair nearby. Then she stood back and stared at the full-bodied Mary in her blue lace-up bodice corselet and her blue stockings and high heels.

Mary stood still for Veronica's slow inspection. First the woman put her fingers on the white flesh just above Mary's stockings. She seemed intent on the spot where Mary's thigh bulged slightly above the patterned stocking top where the suspender curved around.

Then Veronica lifted Mary's left arm and pushed her face into her armpit and inhaled. Then she licked just below the arm before moving her face to be in front of Mary's breasts.

Veronica small stature meant that, in her high heels, her face was inline with Mary's chest. She lifted one hand and her fingers took hold of and fondled a nipple.

Then she took Mary's hand and led her to the bed.

The two hugged and kissed. Both loved kissing and agreed that proper passionate kissing was the key to making love.

"Mary, my sweet darling, I must tell you first that I am blessed with that rare ability to cum pretty much whenever I want to. Right now I really want to sit on your face and cum on your mouth. Can I do that, please? And Mary, I want you to treat me like your sex doll. Anything you want is all right by me. Don't hold back. Let us be lovers to the full. I desperately want to cum all over you."

Mary listened to what Veronica said and joyfully stared at the petite doll-like sex toy nestled in her arms and mentally drooled as she considered just a few of the things she could imagine doing to Veronica.

And, almost as if Veronica had read Mary's mind, the sex doll spoke in a quiet and reassuring voice.

"Oh yes, I forgot to mention that there are sex toys in that draw, dildos large and small. And yes, Mary my love I intend to use them on you and would love you to use them with me. Feel free to shag me with them and send me to heaven, Mary. And it might surprise you, but even my tiny bottom will welcome your attention.

"And Mary, you will be my sex doll to love and to hold.

It wasn't long before Veronica lifted herself up and swung a leg over Mary's chest. She looked down at Mary lovingly as she moved her perfect little bottom backwards and forwards and side to side over Mary's large bosom. Then she put Mary's arms down beside her and moved up and hovered her little vagina over Mary's mouth. Mary gasped and felt a quiver in her groin.

"Now, my darling. I can cum quickly or slowly and right now I think I want to come slowly. I'm going to rub my wet pussy all over your face. You can lick me and push your tongue or nose into me and when I decide to orgasm, I'll tell my sex slave so that she can grasp me tight and hold me. I would love that.

End

CATCH UP

EROS CRESCENT

No one on Eros Crescent remembers exactly the moment when the words COVID-19 or Corona virus were first uttered in their houses. Needless to say, it would first have been heard on a television report and the importance of the message would have taken a few days to sink in.

The world suddenly changed. Words and phrases like lockdown and self-isolation and social distancing were suddenly in the forefront of all conversations as people enacted the requests of government and the nation to act responsibly to assist in the national objective to achieve what quickly became known as flattening the curve.

For Roger, life couldn't have been less affected. His daily routines required only that he rose from his bed, showered and shaved, ate his breakfast, went for a walk, and made sure he had sufficient pens and paper. Although it did impinge on his new paying project.

He had been asked by Desley to write another booklet similar to the one he'd written for The Club, only this was to be for The Dunking, a venue he had not yet visited or, until now, even heard of.

When Desley explained the concept and related what the setting inside the warehouse was like, Roger was very keen to get started. But the arrival of the virus put an end to that project, at least until further notice.

For Caroline and Jackie and Miranda, staying at home was what they enjoyed anyway, that is when they weren't travelling abroad or window shopping or having coffee in cafe's.

All three women had worked in executive positions in London, but moving overseas brought that era to a close, although they had been invited to join similar companies in Australia.

A top of the range coffee making machine was promptly ordered along with a supply of fair trade East Timorese Maubisse, medium blend. Browsing online shops became the new window shopping.

Instagram took on a new importance as the pandemic took hold around the world. Stories and pictures of people in isolation doing amazing and sometime ridiculous things became the rage. Jackie uploaded hundreds of images of the inside and outside of the house, earning the praise of interior designers and architects.

Helen and her husband Frederico were effected in so far as Freddy's job as a flight controller at the airport was soon to be reduced in the number of hours he worked. However, there was no threat to his income as he was on standby as an essential service. But Helen's work as a freelance Human Resources consultant to industry came to a sudden halt. She embraced online conferencing on Zoom but this was no substitute for real hands-on consulting.

Helen was also restricted in her love life, already reduced as a result of her husbands responsibilities to Helen's two lovers who had inadvertently become pregnant to him.

Sophie and Freya now spent a night a fortnight with Freddy. Unable to visit or have visits from her own lovers, Polly or Celia Ashbee, Helen would just have to manage with her next-door neighbour, Mary. And what looked like the answer to maiden's prayer, The Club had been forced to close.

Mary's only loss of employment was her volunteer job at the Salvation Army Opportunity Shop which she would miss very much. She would also miss her sensual workout with her close friend Janice. But most of all, she would miss her newly found excitement at The Club which she had only recently opened.

Her niece and housemate, Sophie, worked at a horse stud and accepted reduced hours and looked forward to doing baby things at home. Because she and Mary lived next door to Helen and Freddy, the two households would have access to each other when needed. And of course, Freddy was to be the father of Sophie's as yet unborn child.

Alice and Frey both lamented the loss of work in their jobs as school counsellors. They both loved their jobs. Both were pregnant and accepted they would be forced to spend more time at home together.

Like most of the others, they had their favourite sex toys for when they weren't knitting baby clothes or doing jigsaw puzzles. And like so many women in lockdown, they visited female friendly porn sites online. The two decided that they would always share these internet session and happily parked themselves on the sofa, transmitting the websites from their phones to the giant television set via a magic little box. This meant that the images were so big that they felt they were in the same room and this proved most enjoyable on many occasions.

Bertie and Rosa were the older folk who were most vulnerable to the virus. They were happy to be isolated although Bertie complained that he would miss his fortnightly get together for coffee and cake with Freddy and Roger.

Bertie complained that he still had much to say on the subject of breaking down the worlds dependance on the "couples model" as he called it.

"Nothing good will happen while we maintain this ridiculous habit of pairing off for life." Firstly, in over half the cases, it doesn't work and people separated or divorced.

"Secondly, it was obvious that people who stayed in these relationships were deeply frustrated by the repressive demands on them of constantly answering to another person.

"Thirdly, paternity and property ownership where the only reasons this system was maintained and with the likely end of democracy as we know it looming, house prices and pension funds and equity investments were likely to collapse.

"And I haven't even mentioned the problems of religion and religious wars."

Rosa looked at him. She loved him dearly but managed always to call him out.

"You haven't mentioned love once."

"Sex and love are two seperate things, my dear. We both know that."

Most of the close friends and relatives knew that Rosa and Bertie had broken up many years ago and taken lovers. Rosa entered relationships with her close girl friends and occasionally, a man.

Sometime later, she and Bertie got back together as a couple, but both maintained their freedom to embark on other relationships if they so chose, and this arrangement worked very well. It wasn't that they were desperate to take on other romantic adventures, but just knowing that they were free to do so, made the difference. They broke up after almost twenty years and had now been together for nearly fifty years.

"It was a necessary pause," agreed the two of them, lovingly.

The two people that were originally going to be living together but in the end chose not too, were Edith and Jessica. But living at different ends of the same street meant that they would not need to forego their times together. And they, like Maude and the others living in number nineteen, had each other for company if and whenever they wanted.

Edith and Jessica had the boys on hand and could also still get a pizza delivered, although it sometimes took a little longer.

But then they learnt that they would now be sharing the boys with the very sexually active Maude and possibly with the two new girls who moved in to number eleven just before the lock down. Jessica and Edith's plans to invite the new girls in for a pizza, were in hand.

Edith still went for her walk on Mount Eros on most mornings where she usually met her friend Chloe and the two, more than not, would spend loving time together in Chloe's secret cave.

It was thanks to the lockdown, that Jessica met Chloe. Edith had long wanted the two to meet so when was Jessica unable to attend classes she accompanied Edith on her walks.

Jessica and Chloe were instantly friends. Both knew that the other understood Chloe's relationship with Edith. And when the rain fortuitously arrived on their first walk together, all three made haste to the hidden cave and it was only a few minutes before Jessica had Chloe underneath her on the carpet of leaves with Edith dragging first Jessica's then Chloe's shorts and panties off before sitting beside them with her bare breasts available for the occasional grope from both girls.

———

It was Desley who had the most to lose but she wasn't particularly put out. The Club had to close only two short months after opening and only a few weeks after Desley had formed a partnership with her friend Sally who had opened The Dunking venue. The Dunking was closed too.

Desley welcomed the opportunity to take a rest and review everything about the club and the new venture and be ready to make any necessary changes or recommendations to Sally when they eventually reopened.

She and her partner Alvie, lived on the premises. Alvie knew about Desley's dalliances with Roger who she said she also had a soft spot for.

Desley had laughed, saying that now that they had so much time on their hands, she would endeavour to entice Roger to pop in for a threesome if Alvie didn't mind sharing. To which Alvie replied that she wanted first go.

Maria and her daughter Serina were at first, forced to stay home with grandfather Aldo and the boarder, Giorgio. They mostly worked for older people as cooks and housekeepers in the stately home of Vaucluse and Woollahra.

They successfully applied for positions with the council as carers so that they could continue working.

They both had each other and the two live-in men to play with when they felt like it plus a range of toys they enjoyed.

Maud, the owner of the music school and owner of the property at nineteen Eros Crescent found isolation difficult, severely limiting her adventures although she had managed to entertain herself with young Ashton and Damian after the two became suddenly sexually aware after falling prey to pizza nights with Jessica and Edith.

And Sylvia and Stella, the two girl who she had enjoyed briefly when they stayed over on the night of her house warming party, seducing Maude with the help their bunny outfits, had booked in for music classes and accomodation the week before lockdown. Maud reasoned that maybe life wouldn't be too bad after all.

Peoples attitudes were changed in part by the arrival of the pandemic.

Australia was fortunate that it could close its borders and clamp down easily on travel.

Europe was badly affected and Britain failed in the early stages to take action which might have prevented many of the casualties they suffered.

The USA continued to be the sad case that it had slowly become.

Big enough to make loud noises but also it seemed, too big to be able to maintain good democratic government.

It was presided over by a man who couldn't cope with an enemy he couldn't see and he couldn't lash out at, or verbally deride.

The arrival of the invisible virus was to prove his undoing.

Life on Eros Crescent went on. The residents continued to love each other in many different ways and despite the sudden disruption of the pandemic, there was a feeling of optimism in the air.

Babies were on the way and new life called out for new ideas. And new ideas about how society worked were desperately needed.

Cross your sanitised fingers everyone, and hope.

The three volumes of the Eros Crescent series are available at Amazon Books as paperbacks or Kindle ebooks.

CONTACT

Publisher or review enquiries should include your full name and details in all correspondence.

Email address:
admin@richardlee.biz

RICHARD LEE PUBLISHING

Erotic Fiction

The Eros Crescent trilogy in separate volumes - as ebooks or paperbacks:

The Fifi Code
ISBN - 978-0-909431-02-0

Eros Crescent
ISBN - 978-0-909431-05-1

Mount Eros
ISBN - 978-0-909431-08-2

Excerpts from the Eros Crescent series - as ebooks or paperbacks:

Janice: A sexual enigma

Jessica: A young woman's journey

Helen: Enough is not enough

Maria: Always available

Mary: Catching up

The Club: Ladies love it!

Literary Fiction

Australian Short Stories

Available as an ebook or a paperback.

ISBN - 978-0-909431-00-6

Restless: A novel about two young men growing up

in Australia between 1900 and 1936 (Publication date not set.)

Out of Print Titles

Mathematics for Young Children by Helen Western

ISBN - 978-0-909431-01-3

Currajong: For Those Whom Schools Have Failed
by Bruce Wicking

ISBN - 978-0-909431-03-7

The Puppetry Handbook by Anita Sinclair

ISBN - 978-0-909431-04-4

Wordswork by Chris Davidson & Bruce Wicking

ISBN - 978-0-909431-06-8

Sheep Production by Murray Elliott

ISBN - 978-0-909431-07-5

Ducks for Starters: A Practical Guide to
Backyard Duck Keeping by Bruce Wicking

ISBN - 978-1-875207-00-8

Sweethearts by Colin Talbot

ISBN - 978-1-875207-02-2